*A book
is a present you can open
again and again.*

THIS BOOK BELONGS TO

FROM

Thumbelina's SONG

Inspired by Hans Christian Andersen's "Thumbelina"

General Editor
Bernice E. Cullinan
New York University

Retold by
Seva Spanos

Illustrated by
Lydia Geretti Halverson

TREASURE TREE™

World Book, Inc.
a Scott Fetzer company
Chicago   London   Sydney   Toronto

Copyright © 1992
World Book, Inc., 525 West Monroe Street, Chicago, Illinois 60661
All rights reserved. This volume may not be reproduced in whole or in part in any form
without prior written permission from the publisher.
Printed in the United States of America
ISBN 0-7166-1601-7
Library of Congress Catalog Card No. 91-65469
8 9 10 11 12 13 14 15 99 98 97 96

Cover design by Rosa Cabrera
Book design by PROVIZION

One perfect morning long, long ago, when spring was whistling its welcome song throughout the ponds and marshes, all of nature was waiting for the news. The king and queen of the flowers were going to have a child. "Hushhh, hushhh," whispered a gentle breeze, "and watch the lily—for the baby grows within."

As the sun rose high above, the water lily slowly opened its petals to the warming light. In the flower's center stood a prince, as hardy as a hazelnut and handsome as a day in spring. His parents called him Floren. "Such a prince must have the most beautiful princess for his bride," said the wishing tree, lifting its heavy branches to the sky.

Just then, a lark sang clear and sweet in the sunlight. A delicate wind stirred, and soon it gently lowered a wild-flower seed onto a lily pad right next to the prince.

A water beetle brought a cockle shell, and the goldfish dusted it gold. The ladybugs brought violets for a mattress. And for a blanket, they took a petal from the lavender rose.

Underneath the petal, the bees placed the seed that would soon become the princess. Then they sealed the shell's edges with honey. The lily blossom finally closed its petals all around, to hide the secret.

Suddenly, the bullfrogs began to bellow. Some children were coming toward the pond. "What beautiful lilies," a little girl said. "I'll take one home to Mother." The water willows began to weep, and the dewdrops cried, but the little girl didn't notice. She picked the lily with the princess inside!

When the mother saw the flower, she was delighted. "Let's put it in a bowl, right here on my table," she told her daughter. Soon after, as the mother sipped her tea, she noticed that the lily petals were beginning to part. The shell inside opened, and standing within was a beautiful little maiden.

The mother's cry of surprise brought her daughter running back again. "Who are you?" they asked.

"I don't know," the maiden replied.

"Then we'll pick a name for you," the mother said. And they chose *Thumbelina* because she was not even the size of a person's thumb.

"You're such a dear little maiden, Thumbelina," they said. "We love you very much, and we will keep you always."

As the weeks passed, Thumbelina had many visitors. The damsel flies wakened her each morning, and the fairy flies told her stories all afternoon. She especially loved to hear about the beautiful pond from which she had come.

But soon Thumbelina began to grow lonely. Every time she heard a lark singing in the sunlight, she wanted to go home to the pond. Yet she was much too big for her friends to carry, and much too small to walk.

The damsel flies and the fairy flies felt bad for Thumbelina.
They wanted to make her feel better. So they learned this
song from the nightingale and sang it to Thumbelina
each night.

Lullaby and goodnight,
Dream your dreams; make them bright.
Come tomorrow, they'll have flown
Where the wishing tree is known—

Gold of branch, leaf, and limb,
Diamond dewdrops set in
Where all dreams come to rest.
Now, to sleep. Dream your best.

By the time the lullaby was over, Thumbelina was
fast asleep.

One morning, when Thumbelina was all alone, a new maid came into the room and gathered the dishes to wash them. She even took Thumbelina's bowl, never imagining that anyone could be inside. Thumbelina ended up in the kitchen sink, between a plate of toast and an egg cup. "Where am I?" she wondered.

Then Thumbelina saw the most curious animal, almost as big as she was. It had six crooked legs and two long, hairy feelers. And it was coming right toward her!

"Stop, you filthy beast!" cried the house mouse, popping out of the woodwork. She grabbed Thumbelina just in time and leapt behind the wall.

Once they were safe inside the mouse's nest, Thumbelina asked, "My goodness, what was that?"

"A cockroach," the mouse replied. "You must keep away from cockroaches—and houseflies too. In fact, you must stay here with me, where you will be safe."

"Thank you very much," Thumbelina replied, "but I want to go home—to the pond."

"Now, now," said the mouse, "be reasonable. It's dangerous out there! There are mosquitoes and ticks and blowflies, not to mention owls and hawks and people and—oh, no, Thumbelina, you mustn't risk it! You're much too big to avoid being seen, yet much too small to defend yourself. I'm just a teeny thing myself and couldn't help you. Besides, it's nice and cozy right here, where I can introduce you to many new friends.

"You're such a dear little maiden, Thumbelina. I love you very much, and I will keep you always."

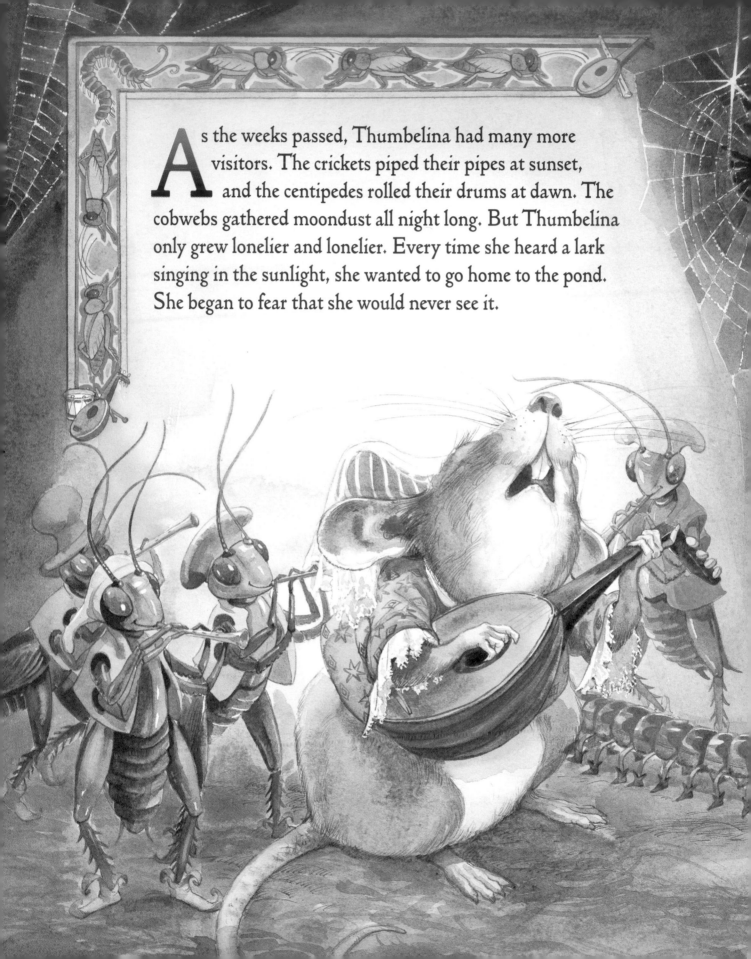

As the weeks passed, Thumbelina had many more visitors. The crickets piped their pipes at sunset, and the centipedes rolled their drums at dawn. The cobwebs gathered moondust all night long. But Thumbelina only grew lonelier and lonelier. Every time she heard a lark singing in the sunlight, she wanted to go home to the pond. She began to fear that she would never see it.

The mouse felt bad for Thumbelina. She wanted to make her feel better. So she learned this song from the nightingale and sang it to Thumbelina each night.

Lullaby, and goodnight,
Dream your dreams; make them bright.
Come tomorrow, they'll have flown
Where the wishing tree is known—

But, for now, stay a spell.
Make a wish. Who can tell?
Nothing's bad as it seems
In a world made of dreams.

By the time the lullaby was over, Thumbelina was fast asleep.

One morning, when Thumbelina was all alone, a garter snake came slithering up to the house mouse's nest. "Who are you?" he asked when he saw the tiny maiden.

"My name is Thumbelina," she replied, "and where did you come from?"

"The garden, of course. If you'd like to see it, just follow me."

And, with Thumbelina holding on to his tail, the snake wiggled and waggled his way through the woodwork and out into a garden full of roses. There, he coiled himself up and fell asleep, leaving Thumbelina on a clump of dirt.

Thumbelina looked up at the long, thorny stems and began to sob. A walking stick had just begun to stare at her curiously when her whole shell began to tip backward. She heard a voice demanding, "What is all this commotion about? And you, you miserable reptile, how many times do I have to tell you not to block my doorway!"

"Don't let him bother you," said the walking stick, stalking away. "He's a trap-door spider, and they're all a bunch of grumps."

"I'm so sorry," Thumbelina apologized, "but I didn't know you were there. The garter snake brought me here and then fell asleep. I'm so alone, and I don't know what to do."

"Well, I reside alone myself, and it doesn't cause me the least bit of anxiety," the spider replied. "Besides, you're well rid of this silly serpent. He's a most preposterous fellow."

Thumbelina became confused by the spider's big words, and she began sobbing even harder. Puzzled, the spider said, "Come now, it isn't logical to flood my house with tears. Instead, why not join me within, where we can discuss your problem and find a proper solution?"

The trap-door spider proved to be very clever, indeed. "Thumbelina," he said, "you are much too big to spend all your time crying like a baby, yet much too small always to act like an adult. Now, you're such a dear little maiden, and I could keep you always, but the best place for you is at home. I say this because I love you very much, and I know how to help you. But you will have to stay with me for just a little while longer."

So Thumbelina remained with the spider. And as the weeks passed, she had still more visitors. The carpenter ants came to measure her from head to toe, and the weaver ants examined her shell closely. The walking stick wrote down all their findings in an important-looking book. The garter snake never really helped, but he popped in his head from time to time to see how things were coming.

Even though Thumbelina's friends tried to cheer her up, she grew even lonelier and lonelier. Every time she heard a lark singing in the sunlight, she wanted to go home to the pond. She could only imagine it, but she loved it all the same.

The trap-door spider felt bad for Thumbelina. He wanted to make her feel better. So he learned this song from the nightingale and sang it to Thumbelina each night.

Lullaby, and goodnight,
Dream your dreams; make them bright.
Come tomorrow, they'll have flown
Where the wishing tree is known—

Over field, brook, and vale,
Where the sweet nightingale
Sings a prayer to the night.
Dream your dreams; you're all right.

By the time the lullaby was over, Thumbelina was fast asleep.

One morning, when Thumbelina was all alone, she dreamed a wonderful dream. A lark had come to take her home. But when she awoke, she saw nothing but the trap-door spider's house.

Then, to her surprise, the trap door flew open. What she had dreamed was true! There was the lark!

According to the spider's plan, the carpenter ants had sawed down some long stems of clover. Then the weaver ants had woven the stems together. Now, around the lark's neck, hung a beautiful swing.

The trap-door spider proudly announced, "This is your way home, Thumbelina!" And as her friends helped her into the swing, the spider bid Thumbelina farewell. "Always remember us, my dear, and the friendship we have shared. Now off to your home at the pond, where someone is waiting to meet you."

The lark burst into song and rose up into the sunlight. Over the fields and meadows she flew, taking Thumbelina home.

By now, the shadows of autumn were sweeping their cool hands across the water lilies at the pond. All the creatures were sad and still. They had long ago given up hope of ever seeing their princess again. They feared she was lost for good.

Suddenly, overhead, the wind brought the sweet song of a faraway lark. As the lark got closer, and her song got louder, the king, the queen, all the animals and flowers—everyone looked up to see. Soon the lark came into sight and gently lowered Thumbelina onto a lily pad right next to the prince.

"Princess May Blossom," he said. "I know you by your golden shell. How I've longed for your return. My name is Floren, and you were meant to be my bride. But you were much too small when you left to remember me."

"Yes," Thumbelina replied, "but I'm big enough now to know that my dreams have come true."

Floren and May Blossom were married under the wishing tree the very same day. No one had ever seen such a celebration. The whirligigs danced, the butterflies swayed, and the fireflies lit up the pond as Floren and May Blossom promised to keep each other always.

And so they did, from springtime till autumn, and from autumn till spring. You can tell because the celebration has never ended. You can hear it for yourself whenever the pond is bathed in sunlight. And in the moonlight, if you try very hard, you will hear May Blossom singing this song.

Lullaby, and goodnight,
Dream your dreams; make them bright.
Come tomorrow, they'll have flown
Where the wishing tree is known—

Gold of branch, leaf, and limb,
Diamond dewdrops set in
Where our dreams never die.
Dreams come true, by and by.

To Parents

Children delight in hearing and reading fairy tales. *Thumbelina's Song* will provide your child with an entertaining story as well as a bridge into learning some important concepts. Here are a few easy and natural ways your child can express feelings and understandings about the story. You know your child and can best judge which ideas will be the most enjoyable.

Play a recording of the song "Thumbelina" for your child. (Recordings are available in libraries and stores.) Join in as your child claps, dances, and sings with the music.

Thumbelina is set in a world of opposites: little creatures and big people especially. Invite your child to play a game called "Opposites" with you. First collect toys, pictures, or other household items. Together, sort them into groups of things that are big and little, old and new, or fuzzy and smooth, for example.

Make a wish with your child to put in a wishing tree like Thumbelina's. Draw an outline of a tree. Draw or cut out a magazine picture of what you wished for. Glue the picture on the tree.

Have your child look through the story to see where Thumbelina met her different friends. Then play a guessing game, alternating who asks questions such as, "Where did Thumbelina meet the house mouse?" or "Where did Thumbelina meet the trap-door spider?" Find the answers in the pictures. Follow up with a hide-and-seek game. Alternate hiding things about the house and trying to find them.

Role-play *Thumbelina*. For example, tell your child, "You be Thumbelina, and I'll be ——." Enjoy making up your lines and acting out the story together.